I0540805

DOUGLASS

THE LOST AUTOBIOGRAPHY — D. HARLAN WILSON

RAW DOG
SCREAMING
PRESS

Douglass: The Lost Autobiography © 2014 by D. Harlan Wilson
ISBN: 978-1-935738-56-5
Library of Congress Control Number: 2013920631

First Paperback Edition, March 2014

All rights reserved. No part of this book may be reproduced, stored in a retrieval system, or transmitted by any means without the written permission of the author and publisher. This is a work of fiction. Published in the United States by Raw Dog Screaming Press.

Cover Design by Matthew Revert
www.MatthewRevert.com

Headliner No. 45 Font by Kevin Christopher
www.KCFonts.com

Raw Dog Screaming Press
Bowie, MD

www.RawDogScreaming.com

PRAISE FOR THE WORK OF D. HARLAN WILSON

"Provocative entertainment."
—*Booklist*

"A bludgeoning celluloid rush of language and ideas served from an action-painter's bucket of fluorescent spatter."
—Alan Moore

"New bursts of stream-of-cyberconsciousness prose."
—*Library Journal*

"Wilson writes with the crazed precision of a futuristic war machine gone rogue."
—Lavie Tidhar

"Wacky experimental fiction."
—*Publishers Weekly*

"Fast, smart, funny."
—Kim Stanley Robinson

"Pomo cybertheory never tasted so good!"
—*American Book Review*

"Utterly original."
—Barry N. Malzberg

"If reality is a crutch, Wilson has thrown it away."
—*Rain Taxi*

ALSO BY D. HARLAN WILSON

Biographies
Hitler: The Terminal Biography
Freud: The Penultimate Biography

Novels
The Kyoto Man
Codename Prague
Dr. Identity, or, Farewell to Plaquedemia
Peckinpah: An Ultraviolent Romance
Blankety Blank: A Memoir of Vulgaria

Fiction Collections
Diegeses
They Had Goat Heads
Pseudo-City

Nonfiction/Criticism
*Technologized Desire: Selfhood & the Body in
Postcapitalist Science Fiction*

For the Blue Swallow Motel.

"I have said that this mode of treatment is a part of the whole system of fraud and inhumanity of slavery. It is so. The mode here adopted to disgust the slave with freedom, by allowing him to see only the abuse of it, is carried out in other things."

—Frederick Douglass, *Narrative of the Life*

CHAPTER 1

Tom Cruise is one of my favorite movie stars and he's a good actor despite the hatemongering of critics and fans that don't like how short and confident he is, but a couch jumper is a couch jumper, and once you jump on that couch there's no jumping off of it: the insurrection sticks to you like a jailhouse tattoo on your face.

For better or for worse, a common misperception is that Tom Cruise started the trend. The fact is couch jumping has existed for centuries. The subject of this autobiography, for instance, former slave and abolitionist Frederick Douglass, was a couch jumper, and a repeat offender to boot, getting overexcited about his mistresses when interviewers brought up the question of his love life.

Of course, screen culture didn't exist in the nineteenth century and written accounts of Douglass's couch jumping didn't hold sway like the real thing.

Douglass: The Lost Autobiography, then, is an epistemology of couch jumping. Originally the book was going to be about Tom Cruise, but there were copyright issues. The next chapter will clarify my modus operandi in more depth and detail.

CHAPTER 2

I mentioned the Dark Hypotenuse, my term for the Lacanian Real, at the end of *Hitler: The Terminal Biography*, and I think I forgot to mention it in *Freud: The Penultimate Biography*. I should say a few words.

Go to chapter three please.

CHAPTER 3

I don't know why my Mini Cooper incites such envy in people. As I have said on several occasions, it is the most expensive model available, and it's a custom-made job. But it's still just a Mini Cooper. You'd think I'm driving around a 20,000-carat diamond, the way some people bark and hoot and cast aspersions at me.

Considering this peccadillo, I have the urge to assign titles to the forthcoming chapters in this genealogy of morals, some of which might sound like this: **Why My Mini Cooper Is So Wise, Why My Mini Cooper Is So Clever, Why My Mini Cooper Writes Such Excellent Books, Why My Mini Cooper Is Fatality** . . .

Let me describe the dashboard.

Standard top tier models come with a wood grain finish, but I was quick to point out to the salesman that wood grain finishes—like, say, anything gold-plated—are for rappers and elderly people. I wanted the dash in blackface set against a stainless steel perimeter and no other color in the vicinity but electronic red, including all LED numbers and digits on the stereo. Incidentally, the stereo has no radio and only plays 12" vinyl records that can be loaded twelve at a time into a souped-up turntable and you can even play two or three records at a time, audiomixing tracks at your leisure with the micronautic knobs of an Art Deco equalizer.

When I think about the Mini Cooper's stereo, the dashboard becomes far less interesting. There is a speed-ometer that goes up to 240 mph. There is a hazard button. There are air conditioning vents. There is a horn. There are other fabulous accoutrements. The windows are tinted, though, and nobody can see inside the vehicle but the person driving it, so clearly the body of the car itself is what's making people jealous.

I would describe the body to you but everybody knows what a Mini Cooper looks like.

CHAPTER 4

Beneath her dress she is entirely naked.

This digression may seem trivial but it is mortally essential. In order to understand the present work, you must come back to this chapter at least every five pages and remind yourself of its existence and importance. The first sentence is the linchpin. This is chapter 4. You might consider writing down the first sentence on a slip of paper and using it as a bookmark so that you don't have to go backwards all the time.

CHAPTER 5

Just as I am a direct descendant of James Fenimore Cooper, author of the Leatherstocking series and so forth, so was Isaac Hayes, author of *Hot Buttered Soul* and *Black Moses* and so forth, a direct descendant of Frederick Douglass. In order to call attention to their relationship, Hayes wore a robe of chains on his bare black body during concerts in the 1970s. In order to call attention to my relationship with Frederick Douglass, I proposed to my publisher that I get naked and wear a similar robe of chains for my author photo, but the editor-in-chief didn't like the idea; in fact, she liked the idea even less than the guiding light and protagonist of my first biography, *Hitler: The Terminal Biography*. So my author photo is just the usual bullshit (check it out on page so-and-so at the end of the book). Nobody gets everything that they want.

Don't forget to go back to chapter 4 and read it again.

CHAPTER 6

I'm going to write this biography slower than the first two. You'll be able to tell the difference. It's harder than you think to write fast and not plan or care about anything. I'm already going faster than the concatenations of my desires would have me go.

CHAPTER 7

Let me provide some context. There's a chance you may not have read the first two biographies in this series. This is a necessity, but I don't blame you for your own deficiencies and limitations. We all have them and I don't judge anybody except in extreme circumstances. Existence is a matter of adaptation and the human condition resists adaptation. Hence sadness.

As you know, I am a professor, author, and body-builder. I hold a Ph.D. in How to Tell the Truth from Zinfandel University, I am an Associate Professor of How to Tell the Truth at the Ludavico Campus of the University of Fostoria, I carved the scikungfi trilogy from the woodblock of my own palsied genius, I placed second on three occasions at the Arnold Classic, and last year I won the Mr. Natural Olympia World Title (in the 40-and-over Master's Division). But there are other concerns here.

For the critical theorist, everything boils down to issues of race, class, gender and sexuality, and ultimately identity. Everything. The same can be said for the nameless Black Hole loitering like an urchin on the street corner. It's egalitarian. It's ungendered. It's Black. It has no identity.

I am that Black Hole. I am that critical theorist.

Remember: chapter 4.

CHAPTER 8

Washington Bailey was being tortured.

The torturer said, "Give us what we want."

Bailey made a face. "No thanks. I think I'll try to Kiefer my way through this." He raised two fingers and put the torturer in a telekinetic death-grip. "Remember, though. I'm letting you do this. Be nice." He lowered his fingers.

Massaging his windpipe, the torturer called his superiors and told them he had a bad feeling.

Everything exploded.

Washington Bailey walked out of the flames and drove to Maryland to see my publisher. Nobody answered the door and he walked around back where the editor-in-chief was weeding the lawn.

"Hi. Hello. Hi."

She didn't hear him so he got down on his knees and started weeding and the editor-in-chief immediately sensed his presence. She got up and went inside to pour herself a glass of lemonade.

A tsunami struck the east coast, leveling the District of Columbia and drowning all of the politicians. Bailey tackled the editor-in-chief and the rest of her family and dragged them to a nearby church just as the tsunami spread across Maryland. They ran up the steeple and hid in the bell tower, crouching in the dark like a family of hunchbacks.

"I guess we don't really have to hide," said the editor-in-chief's husband. "I mean, it's not like the water can see us."

Everybody agreed and then Bailey laid out the terms of his project and delivered the pitch for his new autobiography. "I have written three already," he noted, "but this one will be different. It will begin with a torture scene and involve a tsunami and it will be punctuated by many other cruelties. Like life itself."

The editor-in-chief listened patiently, with a blank expression, like she always did, whether she was listening to a writer's pitch, or a state-of-the-union address, or a stand-up comedy routine, and when Bailey had finished, she expressed various reservations and concerns, but she eventually said they would publish the book, although with virtually no advance and minimal royalties. They had never published one of Bailey's titles before, after all, and she was skeptical about sales returns despite how well his past autobiographies had done, generating hundreds of thousands of dollars in royalties for him alone. That was a long time ago, though, and the publishing world had evolved into a different, dumber animal. Bailey didn't care; after a long sabbatical from the grind of writing, he felt rejuvenated and purposeful and accepted the offer on the spot.

Then the steeple collapsed and all of the bodies sunk into the rubble.

CHAPTER 9

There's a surprise faculty senate meeting in the How to Tell the Truth department at the University of Fostoria's Ludavico Campus.

I haven't been to a faculty senate meeting in three years and should probably go even if it takes me away from my home theater where I do most of my writing and online teaching. But I'm armed with every Angry Birds app on my iPhone and there are still several levels in need of three stars. I also have at least fifty in-progress games of Words with Friends in need of a new move on my end.

Wait.

There's a breaking story on TMZ, my primary source of news. The headline:

TOM CRUISE JUMPS ON COUCH . . . AGAIN

Mark it in your notebook. This chapter was written on the day that TMZ broke the story.

There's no way I'm going to the faculty senate meeting.

CHAPTER 10

Like jokes, anecdotes, and shadows of reality—some chapters are better than others. Content doesn't matter. One chapter will always be better than another chapter, objectively and subjectively. I make no excuses for *Hitler: The Terminal Biography*, *Freud: The Penultimate Biography*, or the present work.

CHAPTER II

I'm having mixed feelings about Tom Cruise's recidivism. On the one hand, it's not a big deal. On the other hand, Cruise apparently jumped off (not on) the second couch in an attempt to commit suicide on Kalypso Shadrach's *Red Sky at Morning Show*, sailor-diving onto the floor. He's in stable condition. Apparently Shadrach made some crass remarks about Scientology and Tom was having a bad day. I like the idea of Scientology, but after all it was created by a sub-par science fiction writer to make money, and the religion involves aliens and thetans and so forth. Still, I felt badly for Cruise and I told my wife, who's always harping on me to express my feelings more often. Not only did she lack sympathy, she said Cruise got what he deserves.

Harsh judgment. She doesn't understand the plight of the celebrity. Movie stars in particular must negotiate flows of desire and *modes de vie* that most of humanity couldn't possibly fathom. Empathy is effectively a fiction. There are only so many movie stars. The rest of us just try to keep up. Or keep out.

CHAPTER 12

Sidebar:

I got my daughters some rubber chickens today at the grocery store and they really took to them. The Bee Gees were playing in the car on the ride home and the girls moved the rubber chicken's arms up and down like Travolta in *Saturday Night Fever*. After awhile they wanted to know if "real chickens" could dance in "real life." I couldn't rightly say no. But I didn't want to lie either. So I told them chickens do in fact dance. "They just don't know they're doing it," I added.

Next chapter.

CHAPTER 13

The year that I'm writing this book marks my publisher's tenth anniversary. They want to give the business a facelift. It will involve revamping their website, hiring more publicity officers, shifting around investments, etc. It will also involve, as the editor-in-chief explained to me, "cutting all dead weight from the roster. We aren't fucking around anymore." I told her that was a good idea and volunteered to deliver the news personally to the dead weight in question. She sent me a list. It took a few months because I had to fly around the country and to England. Now I'm back in my home theater watching a Christopher Meloni marathon and all of my publisher's guns are locked and loaded. They currently work with one author and have no intention of taking on anybody new. "Ever," my contract says. (FYI neophyte writers. This is a unique situation and I don't take it lightly, although I try to be humble about it and occasionally I rely on the social crutch of self-effacement, which allows me to momentarily disavow such ascendancy and solipsism-made-flesh. As I have mentioned before in some capacity, without feeding ourselves regular portions of disavowal, the psyche would implode and we would no longer be able to distinguish the film from the reel.)

CHAPTER 14

Bodybuilding is a seminal element of the Angry Black Author trilogy; in its absence, the trilogy would be something altogether different and certainly inferior. In *Hitler: The Terminal Biography*, I discussed optimum weightlifting and cardio training techniques as well as proper diet. In *Freud: The Penultimate Biography,* I elaborated on diet (namely the importance of hitting your macros on a regular basis and eating whole foods only). Here I need to discuss another aspect of bodybuilding: the toxin of perception.

Perfection is impossible. Whatever the person, place, thing, event or circumstance—nothing is ever perfect. Everything can always be made better.

With one exception. Which renders everything an exception, if properly installed.

In order to obtain the perfect physique, you must murder your soul. And the soul is the engine of the toxin of perception.

Hence the way to accomplish soul murder is to murder perception, i.e., to "allow" oneself to view the imperfections in everything, i.e., in every *body*. This is merely a process of seeing objects as they actually exist in the world rather than seeing them as you have been constructed to see them (and disavow them). Every aspect of every single thing is imperfect, but culture and the psyche train us to see objects and ideas AS THEY ARE NOT for a variety of reasons, among them self-tolerance and self-aggrandizement, e.g., we delude ourselves into thinking our bodies don't look as bad as they do or that somebody else's body looks worse than ours when in fact our bodies are distinguished by an excess of fat cells and look far worse than the human counterparts we finger.

Nobody can deny that I am as a shredded and vascular as I can possibly be. Deny it and you will instantly brand yourself as a *winzige Menschen*.

At the same time, nobody can ever be shredded and vascular enough.

If perfection exists, it is only in the moment, the moment frozen in amber, without the prospect of a future where that which is perfect might be improved upon.

Seeing time is a vital component of seeing the body.

See the body clearly and you will not be able to resist the process of perfecting it and the chronic acknowledgment that perfection is an illusion. The idea is to wrangle and harness the power of desire (bearing in mind that desire, as Lacan reminds us, amounts to *the desire for desire*). Then aim it at your beer belly and pull the trigger. It's an automatic firearm and now you should possess unlimited ammunition.

If the soul is the engine of perception, the body is NOT the prison of the soul. The body is the DREAMWORLD of the soul, an image the soul cast onto the White Canvas, a projection of the soul's fears and desires and crepuscular eccentricities. On the surface, this notion contradicts what I said in past biographies about the soul and the body.

We never leave the surface. There is nothing beneath it. No organs in the body. No pulp in the fiction.

Murder perception and you will murder the soul. Murder the soul and the body will belong to you alone.

At this point, you might benefit from going back to chapter 4 and reading it again. This is the last time I'll mention it. I'll assume you'll continue to go back there throughout the book.

CHAPTER 15

Bram Stoker is a better name for a bodybuilder than an overrated prolix writer. Consider the phonetics. Bram as in Bicep. Stoker as in I Stick the Fucking Pose.

(Revert to chapter 4.)

Bram Stoker went to a BW3's. It was his cheat day.

(Eating massive quantities of both processed and unprocessed foods during the bulking stage is practiced by many bodybuilders, even competitors with their IFBB Pro cards, despite wreaking havoc on your body in the long run, and sometimes the short run. It's better to stay in decent shape all the time and focus on increasing lean muscle mass during the off-season. Then, two or so months before a competition, focus on cutting by dropping your daily carb intake to below 60 grams. But anything goes on a cheat day. Even if you're on a cut, a cheat day can be useful, as long as you don't go completely hogwild and eat 15,000 calories. Ideally you will only indulge in one or two cheat meals per week whether you're cutting or not. Psychologically, though, it's much easier to set a full day and night aside. It's also good to stay away from shit foods like fried chicken and French fries and basically anything fried and sugar-based and so forth. Eat natural peanut butter and Ezekiel bread and whole wheat pastas with clean sauces and turkey meatballs and turkey bacon and ribeye steaks and white cheese and that sort of thing. Or eat whatever. A cheat day comes only once a week. You should be able to enjoy yourself, if only to curb cravings for the other six days of the week, during which calories should be carefully counted and there mustn't be any cheating.)

Stoker ordered twenty-four hot chicken wings with extra celery sticks and two additional servings of blue cheese dressing. He got a beer too. Dos Equis with lime. He used to drink it as a kid growing up in Palermo. That had been years ago. Decades. He couldn't remember the last time he had drank a Dos Equis. The first sip incited an injurious nostalgia. He wasn't prepared for the mnemonic burden. He broke down and cried like a child. Nobody noticed; everybody assumed he had ordered the hot wings. When the wings actually came out, he began to devour them, sucking the meat from the bones in one ferocious motion of the lips and teeth. Within seconds he was crying twice over—once for the sauce, once for history.

By the time he left the BW3's, he calculated an intake of approximately 4000 calories.

CHAPTER 16

I am painstakingly careful when I open the wine, but somehow I manage to cork the bottle at least once a week. It's as infuriating as it is depressing. I only buy good wine and I don't throw the corked wine out even though I know I will be picking cork out of my teeth for the rest of the week. A solution to the problem would be to stop drinking wine, but that's never going to happen. Another solution would be to only buy wine with twist-off tops, but I don't like any of those brands. Yet another solution would be to ask somebody else to open the wine, but I must be in control of everything, and in any case one of these days I'm going to get through a week, seven days, without corking a bottle. In the meantime I'm a slave to this evil and unfortunate circumstance.

Douglass: The Lost Autobiography promises to include more information about slavery and its evils.

That slavery is and always has been an evil enterprise is self-evident. And yet, corking aside, so many people are and always have been slaves in so many different ways. Consider the various systemic, social, gendered, technological and psychological ways in which we permit and often encourage and facilitate our own subjugation. Ironically, most of us are at our best when we're being treated the worst.

CHAPTER 17

After awhile you forget about blackness. So do I. But we should never forget. Blackness means something.

CHAPTER 18

Every utterance holds the promise of a full-blown soliloquy (in the interests of pedagogy) and I attempt to embed a speech in everything I say, i.e., everything I say, if you listen closely, will manifest, literally, as an *oral presentation* . . .

I found myself in the back yard staring at the rose bushes. I was concerned. There were no flowers. I said, "Do these things work?"

My wife glanced up from the dirt where she was planting thyme. She looked at me as if I were an imposter. "Do they work?" she spat.

"Yeah. You know." I made a blooming motion with my hands and made a blooming sound.

"What the hell is that?"

"I don't know. Do these plants grow flowers? That's what I'm asking."

Blinking at me, she returned to the thyme.

After awhile I went somewhere to give a speech.

"Vehicular narrators are deceptively malicious," I began. "You simply can't rely on them as a source of fidelity and *cogito*. Don't let anybody fool you: getting electrocuted to death really hurts. Then they amputate your limbs, detonate the hydrogen tanks and raid the liquor cabinets. Paraspatial metonymies are only as good as the objects they denote and the chainlinks of coiled signification that extend from their frazzled anuses. Apropos. A state of obsessional neurosis becomes the natural psychological habitat of all thinking men. Women are another matter. I don't pretend to know what's going on in their heads. Recently my own wife yelled at me because I asked her a simple question. Who does that? But we can't neglect the importance of radically asymmetrical physiognomies. Ralph Waldo Emerson possessed a radically asymmetrical physiognomy, for instance." I removed a gypsum bust of Ralph Waldo Emerson from a suitcase and placed it on the lectern. "See?" I gestured at the face, then put the bust away. "I know what you're thinking: everybody dies. It's true. *Le grand mort*! A difficult concept to fathom. It can only be a concept; the reality of death, the literal demise of corporeality and consciousness, renders nil the powers of conception. I explained this once to a beer hall of Rotarians. Ha! They didn't want to hear it in spite of repeated assurances that I was a Republican and owned several fancy-looking guns. In retrospect I fear that my use of the phrase 'fancy-looking' may have functioned as an adverse telltale. You folks here at the AARP wouldn't know much about it. Time flies like an archangel's death-dart. Let's see. Primordial acts of affirmation. Also, mortar. Finally, in the words of Jacques Lacan, '*Woman does not exist.*' That's not as bad as it sounds. Remember: the phallus, harrowed by biological and socio-symbolic complexes, is always-already a conscientious objection. *Pas toute.* Thank you for having me. Thank you. Ok."

I walked offstage. The director stopped me and said that I hadn't talked about my books yet.

"Oh yeah."

I returned to the lectern.

"Hello. Caleb tells me I didn't say anything about my most recent publications. He's absolutely right. We can attribute this to my mnemonic shortcomings. Well. I'm the author of the Angry Black Author trilogy. Thank you. Thank you. Thank you. Thank you. Thank you. Thank you. Thank you. Thank you. Thanks. Thank you. Thanks. Thanks. Yep. Thank you. Ok. Ok that's enough. Enough. THAT'S FUCKING ENOUGH!!! Thank you. In order of appearance, the Angry Black Author trilogy includes *Hitler: The Terminal Biography*, *Freud: The Penultimate Biography*, and *Douglass: The Lost Autobiography*. We're currently in the middle of the third and final installment. I have already read you an excerpt, of course; whatever I say is part of the excerpt. Ha! Thank you. Thank you. Thanks. Questions? Yes. You. Yes ma'am. Why did I write the Angry Black Author trilogy? Good question. More? More? Any other questions ok fine no more questions then. At your leisure please take a chance to visit my publisher's website. You might as well write it down. Get out a pen and some paper. That's fine. Yes, you can use a napkin. Does everybody have a pen? No? Can somebody give her a goddamn pen? None of you dumbasses has an extra . . . oh good. The address for my publisher, Raw Dog Screaming Press, is as follows: W. W. W. Dot. R. A. W. D. O. G. S. C. R. E. A. M. I. N. G. Dot. Com. Yes. Com. C-O-M. Again? All right. W. W. W. Dot. R. A. W. D. O. G. S. C. R. E. A. M. I. N. G. Dot. C. O. M. Got it? C . . . O . . . M. Not N. M. Yes. Yes, COM means 'commercial.' No. I don't know what WWW means. It doesn't really matter. Anyway Raw Dog Screaming Press publishes several authors who work out with weights on a regular basis. They're worth checking out. Even some of their out-of-shape authors are pretty good . . ."

CHAPTER 19

Bram Stoker decides to run for President.

"What kind of asshole wants to be President?" says his father, bemused.

"This kind." Bram slowly lifts his arms overhead and strikes a dramatic vacuum pose.

Dad nods. "Shit boy well I just know you're gonna win now. I just know it. You will be the next President of the United States. There's no way you can lose. Soon you will be the commander-in-chief. I might start smoking smokes and drinking drinks again just to celebrate your certain victory. Well let's drink a drink anyway. One for you and one for me. Bottom's up. Mm. My son the goddamn President. Congratulations Mr. President."

Bram loses the election.

"What kind of asshole loses the election?" says his father, enraged.

"This kind." Now Bram strikes a crab pose, foregrounding an impressive set of traps.

Dad nods. "Shit boy well I just know you're gonna win now. I just know it . . ."

CHAPTER 20

"Jesus," my daughter echoes.

"No. People don't like that, honey," I explain. "Say geez. G-E-E-Z."

"G-E-E-Z? What's that mean?"

"It means: Boy oh boy! It means: Goodness gracious! It means: Oh my gosh! It means: Holy cow!"

She laughed and laughed.

CHAPTER 21

In today's publishing industry, writers are often responsible for doing a lot of their own promotional work. Even some major publishers expect writers to carry most of the load. In some cases, publishers will do nothing but publish the book, which, thanks to contemporary printing technologies, can be accomplished at a very low cost. The writer, then, must take care of everything else at his or her own expense (e.g., sending out review copies, setting up interviews, setting up book signings and readings and radio and TV spots, blogging and social networking, etc.). Frederick Douglass was trying to do just that, but somebody from the First International Congress of Gynecology and Obstetrics kept interrupting him, sending him a steady torrent of emails, and every time a new one landed in his inbox, it was accompanied by a loud dinging noise. The dinging noise didn't stop even when he muted the volume on his computer.

"*Das Ding*," Douglass pronounced.

Most of the emails were garbled and unreadable, but he could read a few of them. Here's the last one he received. (Improper use of punctuation, omission of direct articles, and other mechanical errors have been retained for effect.)

Dear Frederick Douglass,

I apologize for the inconvenience if the letter disturbed you more than once. I'm writing to follow-up my last invitation as below, would you please give me a tentative reply? Thank you very much.

On behalf of organizing committee of the 1st International Congress of Gynecology and Obstetrics(ICGO-2012), I would like to invite you to join us and give a speech about **Breast Cancer...** at the session of **STREAM 3-1: Breast Cancer.** It will be held on December 2-4, 2012 at Guangzhou Baiyun Convention Center with a theme "*New Horizons in Women's Health*".

ICGO-2012 is contributed to all the professionals in the field of Obstetrics & Gynecology, where you will have the opportunity to learn about new developments from influential, internationally renowned scientists and clinicians. It is also an opportunity to share aspects of your

own work by submitting a poster or oral presentation. The scientific program has a lot to offer the
different subspecialties in our discipline and also
covers general topics which will be of interest to
many. The meeting will provide an opportunity
for networking with colleagues and catching up
with old acquaintances.

To join the post-conference tour, you will
have the opportunity to experience some of the
South China's best attractions as well as learning
about the city's captivating history.

I hope you will come to and contribute to
what we predict will be a highly successful and
stimulating Congress. Welcome you to log on the
website to learn more details about the conference.

Your prompt reply with a speech proposal
will be highly appreciated.

Best regards,
Ms. Cathy Wang

"That's going in my lost autobiography," Douglass
pronounced. It did, after all, happen to him.

CHAPTER 22

It is no small coincidence that Frederick Douglass also holds a Ph.D. in How to Tell the Truth, although he received an honorary, posthumously awarded degree, whereas it took six years of concentrated study at Zinfandel University in Switzerland to acquire mine.

Every truth has the structure of fiction. Thus Douglass and I are as much truth-tellers as storytellers. Even the strictest modes of criticism and historical research bear the mark of fiction. It's impossible to escape. Whether we like it or not, our imagination is the filter through which we perceive and represent the objective world. Fantasy structures reality through the vehicle of desire. Thus spake Žižek via Lacan.

In other words, our Ph.D.s in How to Tell the Truth are by default Ph.D.s in creative writing. Useless in other words. Gratuitous at best.

A M.F.A. (Master of Fine Arts) in creative writing is a terminal degree according to plaquedemic scripture. Curiously, plaquedemia seldom acknowledges the M.F.A. degree as such, and the recipient of the M.F.A. degree experiences chronic difficulty landing a fulltime teaching position, let alone a tenure-track job at a reputable university, or any university. Most M.F.A.s find themselves teaching adjunct classes while publishing a story or book here and there. In almost every case, financial returns are nominal, even with Big Six publishers.

What, then, is the use-value of the Ph.D. in creative writing? There are not many programs of this kind in the United States. But they exist.

The student who goes on for a Ph.D. in creative writing does so because s/he's scared of getting a fulltime job, or scared of not getting a fulltime job, or merely uninformed, or not intelligent and hardworking enough to get a Ph.D. in a real, rigorous field (e.g., philosophy, English, How to Tell the Truth), or unable to complete a book-length manuscript beyond the scope of a "dissertation" (if they ever even complete the "dissertation"), or totally and foolishly and incorrectly elitist, or some amalgam of the aforementioned infirmities.

In the end, one should not spend the time and money required to get a M.F.A. or Ph.D. in creative writing unless one is independently wealthy, comfortable with permanent indigence, or capable of maintaining a hearty belief in the Dangling Carrot that is the American Dream for the duration of their lives. Carrots, dangling or otherwise, possess more carbs than you think.

Now let's put Frederick Douglass and Bram Stoker in the same room and see what happens.

CHAPTER 23

I have decided to write only about motels from now on.

Motels are interesting enough.

There is an abundance of rooms that you can go in and go out of and each room contains a unique slice of life.

Additionally, I won't have to invent new settings and you won't have to figure out the new settings I invent. Everybody wins.

Let's start at the Blue Swallow Motel in Tucumcari, New Mexico. Let's end there too.

Here's a description of the Blue Swallow I discovered in *USA Today* in an article entitled **10 great places for a quirky night's sleep**. I usually only get my news from TMZ, but sometimes I rip through all of the stories and need something else to do while I eat breakfast (almost invariably eggs and berries; sometimes I sprinkle grated cojack cheese on the eggs and include a side of low-sodium turkey or chicken sausage). The description reads:

> Travelers on a Route 66 pilgrimage are drawn to this motor court for its neon sign. The image of a fluttering bird and the promise of "100% Refrigerated Air" have been luring motorists off the Mother Road since 1939. Inside, the rooms offer vintage lighting, period furniture, and rotary phones. The building is on the National Register of Historic Places.

Sounds like utopia to me. Again and again, reality proves itself to be better than fiction even as fiction flexes its muscles and prances across the stage of reality like a bedevilled continuum.

CHAPTER 24

I left my home theater to go out and get some cigarettes and tilapia between chapter 22 and 23 and forgot about Douglass and Stoker. Tilapia contains a lot of protein. Fish is in fact the highest quality protein source (especially white fish). Don't worry. We'll come back to Douglass and Stoker. Their interaction may work particularly well considering that we've got the motel on our side.

CHAPTER 25

Here is a brief deviation before we get started with the motel subterfuge. If it bothers you just pretend this chapter is enclosed in parentheses. All of the chapters in *Douglass: The Lost Autobiography* (as well as, for that matter, *Freud: The Penultimate Biography* and *Hitler: The Terminal Biography*) are technically enclosed in parentheses anyway.

I was in the bookstore. The Waterstones in Piccadilly Circus. They have a strong selection of Lacan translations. Also they have good lemon bars in the café. I like to eat one or two lemon bars on cheat days.

I strolled down the aisles wincing at bad book titles and ugly book covers as I ate my lemon bar. Somebody saw me making faces and approached me. A woman. Middle-aged. Not unattractive. But not worth a double-take.

"That's my book," she said.

Pretending not to hear her, I winced harder.

"That's my book," she reiterated. "I wrote it."

"This one?" I yanked the book off the shelf, laughed at it, breathed on it, dropped it on the floor, and stomped on it as hard as I could.

"Oh my god!"

She recovered the book and shouted for a security guard. The guard came over and the alleged author told him what happened, cradling the book like a wounded infant.

We went back and forth for a few minutes. I exhibited my proverbial mutant calm. In the end I was presumed innocent. I even managed to finagle a free lemon bar out of the episode.

CHAPTER 26

Moral: you are not special.

If we realized this confounding truth, if we came to terms with the zero-degree nature of our existence, the world would be an unrecognizably different place. Only at the nadir of enlightenment can we assemble a selfhood (or, if you prefer, "cell-hood") that puts us in a position to achieve, as French schizoanalysts Gilles Deleuze and Félix Guattari suggest, "that glacial reality where the alluvions, sedimentations, coagulations, foldings, and recoilings that compose an organism—and also a signification and a subject—occur."

I am no exception.

CHAPTER 27

Recently I have been experiencing the Dread. It never lasts long. No more than a few seconds, sometimes. But those are potent seconds.

Only last year did I determine the origin of the Dread. Airplanes.

In the weeks before a flight, the Dread creeps up on me and gets worse and worse. On the plane, I drink screwdrivers and feel relaxed, even happy. In the weeks after the flight, the Dread slowly dissipates and goes away, like a wound in my sensorium healing over. Then, when I have to take another flight, it's like the wound is torn open, and the cycle starts again. As I mentioned in other biographies, I used to take anxiety medication (e.g., Ativan and other benzos). They worked like a charm, but the rebound anxiety was too powerful and freaked me out even more than the Dread. Now I just carry around these vials of patchouli and clary sage that my wife gave me. I sense the Dread on the periphery and I open the vials and sniff them. Occasionally I dab the substances onto my overlip and the rims of my nostrils. Aromatherapy. It works, sort of. But it requires constant mindfulness and vigilance.

Solution: don't fly.

Problem: book tours require me to travel all over the world on a regular basis. I'm in Kowloon right now preparing to do a reading from *Hitler: The Terminal Biography* this evening at Kubrick's Yau Ma Tei branch. Thursday I have to be at The Bam Bookshop in Cape Town on behalf of *Freud: The Penultimate Biography*. So forth.

At any rate, I refuse to be one of those aerophobes who doesn't fly anywhere because he's afraid of blowing up in mid-air when a bomb goes off in the lavatory or a spark gets into the gas tank or another plane rams into you.

We should go to the motel now.

CHAPTER 28

A boy stands on the roadside. He can't be more than five or six years old. He appears to be selling something. Not lemonade. The red wagon is empty. He looks confident. Behind him is the Blue Swallow Motel. Above him is an oblique neon sign that reads 100% REFRIGERATED AIR and VACANCY and TV! and HISTORIC PROPERTY and TRUCK RV PARKING.

CHAPTER 29

They make a mistake and check Frederick Douglass, Bram Stoker and Immanuel Kant into the same room. The motel is at full capacity. Everybody must adapt to the situation.

The articles of historicity stand between the beds.

It's awkward. There's a language barrier. Kant only speaks German and Stoker's Irish accent is thick as molasses. Also Kant can't be bothered with Stoker and his fuckin' vampires and white worms and so forth. Douglass feels weird, but he always feels weird around white folks, even after all these years.

This goes on for awhile and then Kant finds some complimentary whiskey. They do a shot. They do three more shots and everybody loosens up. Sipping the whiskey now, they turn on the refrigerated air and turn on the TV and check the shower pressure and make plans to survey the historic property and have a cookout in the RV park in the not-too-distant future.

CHAPTER 30

Did you like how I put Kant in that room with Douglass and Stoker too? Did you like that? It's all right: everything points back to Kant. Nothing really existed before Kant. Now go to the next room. And go back to chapter 4 if you haven't already.

CHAPTER 31

Alois Villafuerte quit his job as the Boss and went to the Blue Swallow Motel to get away from all of the exploding airplanes. He had seen enough airplanes explode in his time and he resented being extinguished as a character and human being at the end of *Hitler: The Terminal Biography*. But as the song says you can't keep a good man down.

He checked in to a room and the room exploded just as he was unpacking his suitcase, with visions of a hot shower, of a deep sleep on a clean bed flickering across his mindscreen. He stood there in the ruins, blackened, dead once and for all, never to return to the symbolic order or any other order. It was a sad day for everybody.

CHAPTER 32

Alois Villafuerte knew that the motel was going to explode just as one knows that one is in the middle of a dream but can do nothing to make oneself wake up.

The motel exploded.

He called the airport and asked if he could have his job back. They said they had hired somebody else to be the Boss and anyway AirFreud had found a way to more or less conduct its affairs without human mediation and intervention. "The planes have learned how to think," they said, "which means they've learned how to kill themselves."

Villafuerte thought he would go back to work anyway. He got into his car and drove to work and pulled up in front of the motel.

He went inside and pounded the dinger. A man with a stubbled, stuck-open mouth appeared from the back room and fell down. He got up and fell down again and got up and said, "I fell down a couple times right there." He pointed at the floor.

"This isn't an airport," said Villafuerte.

The manager gave him a key. Room 56.

Villafuerte drove around the motel looking for room 56. He couldn't find it. The key exploded. He went back to the front desk and the manager gave him another key. Room 23. "I didn't fall down," he said proudly.

"I'm going to work," said Villafuerte.

"What sort of work do you do?"

"Industry. Business. Commerce. Engineering. Production. Supervision. Regulation. Administration."

"That sounds like something. Good, like."

He drove around the motel looking for room 23. He couldn't find it. The key exploded. He went back to the front desk and the manager gave him another key. "The third key," he droned. There was no number on it.

He found the room immediately and a mariachi band ambled around the corner of the pink stucco building and started to play something.

Villafuerte paid them to be quiet and went inside.

CHAPTER 33

A masseuse awaits Alois Villafuerte like a wuxian geisha, arms and legs poised at the ready.

She wants to give him a hot stone massage.

Villafuerte says ok but he has to use the toilet so he goes into the bathroom and he stays in there for awhile. He doesn't know if he wants the masseuse to go away or not. A hot stone massage sounds good. But the context is out of whack. He hasn't bought a hot stone massage, after all, and he doubts that the rooms at the Blue Swallow Motel include complimentary hot stone massages.

He decides that he doesn't like the Blue Swallow Motel. The floor is kind of dirty and the walls are cheap-looking and the shower mat is made of paper. Also the quilts on the beds have tacky designs, the window treatments belong in an Old Folks Home, and there's a giant oil painting of a weathered Native American chief over the bed. And then this masseuse. The place looked ok from the outside but now that he's gotten to know it a little better it's a big letdown.

Well I might as well get that hot stone massage, he tells himself.

He flushes the toilet and washes his hands and exits the bathroom and there's the masseuse waiting with the stones in her hands. She's taken off most of her clothes and her skin is smooth and dark and her curves fit together in all of the right places. He's had plenty of hot stone massages before. To make her comfortable, he tells her that he's never had a hot stone massage and she assures him sir you're going to like this hot stone massage.

He takes off his clothes and lies facedown on the bed. The masseuse puts a towel over his back and legs and starts to massage him with the stones.

"Ouch!" he says. The stones are too hot. The masseuse apologizes and starts again.

"Jesus!" he says. The stones are too hot. The masseuse apologizes and starts again.

The stones explode.

Alois Villafuerte takes the masseuse in his arms and they roll into one another. He figures it's time to make love to her. He removes a prophylactic from his wallet and the prophylactic explodes. "It's a good thing I didn't put that prophylactic on," he tells the masseuse. But she has melted into a fuselage of permanence.

CHAPTER 34

I don't feel like writing another chapter right now. I'm going to cut and paste my story "The Arrest" into *Douglass: The Lost Autobiography*. Call it a reprint. "The Arrest" may also be found in my fiction collection *They Had Goat Heads* (Atlatl Press 2010). I sent out the story for publication in magazines and journals before its appearance in *They Had Goat Heads* and everybody rejected it with vehemence. Then, when *They Had Goat Heads* came out, "The Arrest" received widespread acclaim from readers and critics alike. Even a number of editors and publishers wrote me and told me how much they liked it and wanted to anthologize it. That's the way it goes sometimes. It's not the only story of mine that's met with the same fate.

Note the story's main theme: the absurdity of patriarchy and male power-relations. Also note the way in which this theme functions as a metaphor for *Douglass: The Lost Autobiography* vis-à-vis the "shackles" or "chains" that bind the masculine subject to the slavemaster of desire.

As a matter of context and relevance, I require that you pretend "The Arrest" takes place in a room at the Blue Swallow Motel.

And now: "The Arrest."

The Arrest

A man said, "You are under arrest."

Another man said, "No. You are under arrest."

"No," said the first man. "It's the other way around. You are the one who is under arrest."

"I'm not under arrest," said the second man. "You are."

"I'm going to arrest you now," said the first man, taking the second man by the elbow.

"No. Now I will arrest you," said the second man, taking the first man by the elbow.

"Let go of my elbow," said the second man. He agreed to let go, but only if the second man let go too.

A third man said, "I'm putting the two of you under arrest."

"No," said the first man.

"No," said the second man.

"Yes," said the third man.

The first man put the third man in a headlock.

The third man jumped up and down and the third man groaned perfunctorily.

The second man put the first man in a headlock. He jumped up and down so that the third man experienced the brunt of two men jumping up and down. He groaned louder, with more drama, yet with less resolve.

"That's enough," said a fourth man. "You are all coming with me. You are all under arrest."

The second man tried to put the fourth man in a headlock with his free arm but the fourth man ducked out of the way. A fifth man snuck up behind the fourth man, wrapped his hands around his neck and choked him to death. Eyes wide with surprise, the fourth man slid to the floor like a raw egg.

The second man released the headlock on the third man. The first man released the headlock on the second man. The first, second and third men faced the fifth man and the third man said, "You killed that man."

"The three of you are under arrest," said the fifth man.

A sixth man punched out the fifth man. "I'm arresting you." He looked askance at the other men. "I'm arresting all of you too."

The second and third men attacked a seventh man with tomahawks before he could open his mouth and put anybody under arrest. The seventh man shrieked during the murder. Blood exited his wounds in japanimated spurts as he accused the first and sixth men of allowing him to be murdered by the second and third men.

Weird mucous leaked from the fifth man's pyretic orifices.

With his last breath, the seventh man whispered, "I should have arrested you all."

Unexpectedly, the first man took off his clothes and began to make love to his wife. She lay on a cot, on her back, beckoning him with spread legs and locked knees.

"What does he think he's doing?" asked the third man. The fifth man woke up and the sixth man punched him out again, dirtying his fist with slime. The third man said, "Public sex is an offense. I'm putting those sex offenders under arrest."

The first man climbed off his wife and attacked the third man. They wrestled around on the floor. The nakedness of the first man made the third man increasingly uncomfortable, and he tried his utmost to beat and arrest his opponent without touching him, an impossible feat, technically, and yet within moments, he was in fact beating his opponent without touching him, somehow, impressing all of the other men, except for the second man, who turned to the sixth man and told him that he knew how to beat people up without touching them better than the third man did.

Soon the first man rallied. He grabbed the third man by the ears and cranked his head and snapped his neck. The third man slumped over like a wet pancake. The first man immediately arrested him. Then he arrested the fourth man, the fifth man and the seventh man.

"You can't arbitrarily arrest dead men," said the sixth man.

"You can't arrest an unconscious man," said the second man.

"I can arrest just about anybody I want," said the first man.

"No. I can arrest just about anybody I want," said the second man.

"No you can't," said the sixth man. "I can. I can arrest anybody. I can arrest the entire world."

"I'm putting the world under arrest," said the fifth man, awakening.

"No. I'm putting the world under arrest," said the sixth man. He blew off the second man's head with a shotgun. "I'm going to arrest the galaxy as well." He turned the shotgun on the fifth man and fired. The fifth man's stomach exploded into flaming tendrils of gore. The sixth man said, "Forthwith I will put every last black hole in the universe behind bars. I will teach Eternity the very meaning of deference and respect and authority. But first things first." He emptied the shells from the shotgun, reloaded it, and put the barrel in his mouth . . .

The first man looked at his wife. She was asleep. "Wake up," he whispered helplessly. "You are under arrest."

She opened her eyes. She stretched, sighed.

She rolled off the bed, slipped into the bathroom and turned on the shower, annulling the voice of her husband . . .

CHAPTER 35

Still in the motel. Go to chapter 4. Then to chapter 36, viz., room 4.

CHAPTER 36

Somebody sits at a desk in room 4 and writes the following note on Blue Swallow letterhead: "I am the author of the novel *I Will Turn Your Face to Alabaster*. I am also the instigator of chapter 42 in *Hitler: The Terminal Biography* in which a character named "Alois Villafuerte's doppelgänger" must endure the repeated transformation of his face into alabaster. This is not a coincidence. I . . ."

The writer is too heavy and the back legs of the chair break, spreading his body across the carpet and the cinderblocks. We don't know if he lives or dies.

The note stays where it lays, forever unfinished.

CHAPTER 37

End vignette.

I miss the characters from *Freud: The Penultimate Biography*, especially the Wolfman and Donovan Ogg. I don't remember any of the characters in *Hitler: The Terminal Biography*. One of them had a funny name, I think.

Commence disaster scenario.

Contrary to popular belief, a falconer is neither somebody who mimics or parodies falcons nor somebody who hunts and kills falcons with a gun. Rather, a falconer is somebody who hunts and kills falcons with another, meaner falcon.

Introjection.

Eisegesis.

Endopsychic allegories are not as overrated as coded celebrations of nomenclature. And pat steampunk dreams smell more like aborted Abscam than burnt oil.

Purchase zodiac.

Any authentic rap song can be traced back to the spirituals, secular rhymes and ballads of slaves who used these vernaculars as an outlet for the trauma of their bondage when they were working in the ditches and the fields under the blistering sun. Here are the final lines from a ballad entitled "The Signifying Monkey":

Monkey hollered, Ow!
I didn't mean it, Mister Lion!
Lion said, You little flea-bag you!
Why, I'll eat you up alive.
I wouldn't a-been in this fix a-tall
Wasn't for your signifying jive.
Please, said Monkey, Mister Lion,
If you'll just let me go,
I got something to tell you, *please*,
I think you ought to know.
Lion let the Monkey loose
To see what his tale could be—
And Monkey jumped right back on up
Into his tree.
What I was gonna tell you, said Monkey,
Is you square old so-and-so,
If you fool with me I'll get
Elephant to whip your head some more.
Monkey, said the Lion,
Beat to his unbooted knees,

You and all your signifying children
Better stay up in them trees.
Which is why today
Monkey does his signifying
A-*way-up* out of the way.

Begin with a scream. End with the sky. During the steeple-chase, don't fall off the horse.

Revert to ciphers of violence and despair . . .

CHAPTER 38

There's a pool in the shape of a frightened amoeba.

Somebody jumps into the deep end and sinks to the bottom. It doesn't matter what their name is. But let's call them Kobe Bryant.

The bottom of the pool is rough, like sandpaper, and Kobe has callouses and divots on his heels that even No-Crack cream won't assuage, although he's generally impatient and too lazy to apply the cream on a daily basis. But here's this pool floor now.

He swims to the shallow end and sort of sits in the water. Then, one at a time, he rubs his heels back and forth across the floor, swiftly, as if trying to start a fire with sticks, and a flurry of dark, dead skinflakes rises to the surface and surrounds him like a cancerous offal. It's pretty disgusting but he's got to take care of his feet.

The manager comes out and shoots Kobe. He misses.

Kobe continues to sand his heels. He wants to finish and he's been shot at before. He's used to it.

The manager takes close aim, steadies his breath, and fires off another round. He misses again.

"I'm almost done!" exclaims Kobe.

Irked, the manager limps to the edge of the pool's widest lobe. He's, like, really close. He leans over and rests the barrel of the gun against Kobe's temple. There's no way he can miss now.

He pulls the trigger.

He misses.

"What the fuck!" cries the manager.

Kobe grabs the rifle and throws it in the pool. The manager gets mad, limps back to the main office and calls the police. They show up at once, guns blazing, bullets hissing into the water.

Nothing hits Kobe Bryant.

Out of ammo, the police try to coax Kobe out of the pool. He tells them they can wait. They wait. The manager orders him to stop doing that. Kobe tells him he's a paying guest and he can use the pool just like everybody else. "Yeah but you can't do that," says the manager. "You're getting semen all over the place." Kobe laughs and asks what they think he's doing in there. He explains how that's not semen. It's his feet. Does he really think his semen is that color and that texture? The police intervene to avoid a race riot and they say something like, "Of course that's not semen. We know what a black man's feet look like. Nobody meant to call your feet anything but feet. I don't even know what semen is. Something having to do with grammar? I was very bad at English in school. I know what feet are though. Yessir I know a thing or two about feet."

Still, when Kobe finishes and gets out of the pool, they put him in handcuffs and drag him screaming by the ankles to the police vehicle, covertly admiring the smoothness of his heels.

CHAPTER 39

Somebody said, "I think I hear a race riot outside." They pushed aside the curtain with a finger and timidly peered out the window.

There was a race riot.

It might have been a gender riot.

Or a class riot—proles rising against their evil bourgeois masters.

Or a sci-fi convention gone awry.

There were so many players and they were all different colors and they dressed differently and there were men and women and androgynous-looking people too.

Everybody was upset about something and beating on one another with two-by-fours and crowbars.

Blacks fared better than whites.

Women and androgynes fared better than men.

Proles fared better than Fredersens.

None of the fanboys fought particularly well. But the Marginalized got the upper hand on the Dominant.

Around dinnertime, the hotel manager staggered outside, blasted apart a cloud with a shotgun, and restored order to the Blue Swallow Motel. Everybody apologized and shook hands and lurched and slumped back to their rooms, weapons dragging across the gravel like heavy tails.

CHAPTER 40

I forgot about Washington Bailey. Let's put him in room somethingorother with soandso. Actually no. He should be alone.

Washington Bailey awoke from a bad dream. Not a nightmare, per se. But he forgot it instantly and then he couldn't remember if it was bad or good.

As he brushed his teeth, he remembered a church, and he remembered a terrible cataclysm.

As he took a shower, he remembered how the shadows coalesced into a big-handed giant. This either happened in a nursery or a nursing home. He might have been two. He might have been dead and forgotten.

The room smelled like decayed integers.

As he ate all of the room's complimentary food and drank all of the room's complimentary drinks, he remembered the first rumblings of Pangaea breaking apart. The dinosaurs and the Christians ran for cover but there was nowhere to hide except underneath all of the matriarchs' parasol skirts.

The distant future lapsed into dark matter with a laugh and a choke and an echo.

He once ate a good plum and had never felt better in his life.

And yet everything seemed blurred and lurid. An achromatic, if not violent, convergence of meaning and purpose and energy . . .

But now he had become drunk and his misgivings had deliquesced and evaporated into the refrigerated air. It didn't matter what he could remember and what he couldn't remember.

He unbuttoned his trousers, laid on the bed and stared at the ceiling, perfectly content. If only everything could be this easy.

CHAPTER 41

I'm growing weary of the Blue Swallow Motel, but I need more words if I'm going to hit the 15,000 mark and remain consistent with *Hitler: The Terminal Biography* and *Freud: The Penultimate Biography*. Honestly I'm sick of the entire Angry Black Author modality. Over the past year, I have been working sporadically on a "serious" novel called *Outré* regarding a man, a woman, a skywhale, and a permutation of Herman Melville, but I've temporarily abandoned it for this portico of scars and pedagogies, which, together with *Hitler: The Terminal Biography* and *Freud: The Penultimate Biography*, will generate considerable returns. The University of Fostoria's Ludavico Campus provides me with a generous annual salary, including excellent medical benefits for my family, and I get raises for scholarship (i.e., published criticism and fiction). But as any good *artiste* will tell you, the psyche withers if it doesn't receive constant nourishment and positive reinforcement from its own private signifyin(g) monkey. And my monkey, as I have either asserted or inferred in other fictions, nonfictions, antifictions, outréfictions, cryofictions and superzerofictions, is losing its Kong.

More.

And when in doubt: EXPLODE.

CHAPTER 42

Somebody set a monkey loose at the Blue Swallow Motel.

"Kill the dirty motherfucker!" shouted somebody else.

Everybody stormed out of their rooms and started yelling and chasing the monkey around the pool. None of them had been involved in the poststructuralist riots of chapter 39, although they all looked exactly the same as those rioters down to the shape of the nose, the diameter of the nostrils, and the elasticity of the deconstruction.

The monkey explodes.

This throws everybody out of sync. They don't know what to do.

They explode.

The motel explodes.

But somehow the motel retains its scaffolding and reconstructs itself *in extenso*.

It explodes again.

The manager slinks out of the flames and wonders what the hell is going on and he explodes.

The sun explodes. But not the moon.

Solar flares attack the earth, razing it from pole to pole, and the Blue Swallow Motel is the only thing left, preserved by a containment field bestowed upon it by friendly god particles.

The manager, burning, tries to turn the motel into a slave plantation.

Frederick Douglass intervenes and bashes in the manager's skull with a hunk of asphalt torn from the road.

Only Douglass remains. He gives a speech and the speech explodes. He starts over and the speech explodes again. He applies mindfulness to the situation and takes calculated breaths and starts over one more time and gets about five seconds into the speech before it explodes.

Thoughts explode before they are born. Before their parents and their grandparents are born.

The void explodes. The Lacanian Real a.k.a. the Dark Hypotenuse explodes.

Employing an uncanny will to power, Douglass psycho-kinetically recreates the Lacanian Real a.k.a. the Dark Hypotenuse, then retires to the motel. He can't remember what room he's staying in, and he doesn't want to ask the manager, because everybody knows the manager doesn't like black people, so he strides up to a door and kicks it in.

Splinters spray across the uncured mattress.

He enters the room and the walls crumble into soot.

The entire Blue Swallow Motel mimics the pretense.

The air vaporizes. Douglass can't breathe. He realizes why. He got too close to the Lacanian Real a.k.a. the Dark Hypotenuse. Not only that: he recreated it. That's what happens. Watch any David Lynch movie. Time and again: *the grimace of the Real*. The impossible. The undifferentiated. That without fissure. That which is beyond (or beneath, or between) language. As Lacan himself says: "The domain of whatever subsists outside of symbolization."

CHAPTER 43

Confession.

This is the last chapter in the book.

The last chapter I'm writing.

Like a barcode, my pedagogy is only as good as the product it encrypts.

Every parasentence will manifest as a single paragraph.

I learned this technique from Japanese science fiction author and critic Kawamata Chiaki.

He employs the one-parasentence artifice for effect, among other enterprises.

Time is the slave of space just as space is the slave of time and the mind is the prison of the body and the body is the prison of the mind.

I wasn't sure what to put here.

I waited until I had finished *Douglass: The Lost Autobiography* and then came back.

I'm not sure what to put here.

This is what happens next.

I'm back.

I took a long break between this parasentence and the last parasentence.

I didn't go to the gym.

Nor did I smoke or drink.

I went to see a psychiatrist.

I've never been to a psychiatrist before.

I used to see a behavioral psychologist.

She couldn't prescribe anything.

Basically she talked to me about the brewery her husband owns and different mindfulness techniques.

When your brain is screaming like a sawed-in-half wraith all the time, it's hard to be mindful with any sort of regularity.

My family doctor used to prescribe me drugs.

I haven't seen him in a year or two.

I think I mentioned somewhere, either in *Freud: The Penultimate Biography* or *Hitler: The Terminal Biography*, but I think it was in *Freud: The Penultimate Biography*, not to completely rule out *Hitler: The Terminal Biography*—I may have mentioned that I used to take Lorazepam for anxiety, namely for the existential Dread that accompanies flying, my inability to fall asleep in less than three hours after going to bed (I get insomnia for weeks at a time), and the pointed fear of death that sneaks up on and attacks me without warning.

Just as there is the little other (*autre*) and the big Other (*Autre*), so is there the little fear (*peur*) and the big Fear (*Peur*).

They all matter.

When you possess an oversized ego, it's upsetting to dwell on your consciousness exploding into nothingness.

I tell people I'm an agnostic.

"Anything is possible," I tell them, lighting another cigarette with one hand, accomplishing an additional rep with the other.

Lorazepam (brand name Ativan) was too strong and addictive and fun.

Drugs shouldn't be fun.

They should even you out.

Nothing more.

I took Ativan every night and after awhile I needed to take it every night.

Every morning I experienced rebound anxiety.

I took it on and off for about ten years and when I wasn't taking it I drank on and off.

There's more.

Breathing, I told the psychiatrist everything in about fifteen minutes, a lifetime's worth of stressors and break-downs, episodes and binges, origins and wills to power, bad times and really bad shitstorms, the importance of massive deluges of endorphins to tranquilize my "fleeting-improvised" demons, the respective importance of my pituitary gland and hypothalamus, how I overtrain and try to work out less, to write less (and worse), to find hobbies that don't chronically devolve into "work."

"And so forth," I concluded.

The psychiatrist was nice and looked something like a dispossessed mandrill.

I didn't say anything about him being out of shape.

He made good eye contact when he talked to me.

Most people are afraid of me or get nervous around me and look at my ears or my chin or the ceiling or their toes when they talk to me.

He told me about the different benzos used to treat anxiety and their various lengths and degrees of effect.

"Know thyself," he repeated.

He suggested I give Xanax a try for what he deemed occurrences of "mortal panic," then referred me to a therapist to talk about my insomnia, which, he deduced, was a separate issue.

At last he said, "Come with me."

We pulled up to the Blue Swallow Motel and got out of my Mini Cooper.

Nothing happened.

CHAPTER 44

Note to Self:

The original title of the arcade game Donkey Kong, regarding the adventures of a large gorilla and a small Italian mechanic, was, not inappropriately, MONKEY KONG. Created by Japanese wonk Shigeru Miyamoto, the game was mistranslated into English. By the time somebody discovered the mistranslation, millions of labels had already been printed.

CHAPTER 45

More and more fiction writers have been instigating Kick-starter campaigns to "subsidize" their "work," i.e., they don't have any money (*quod negotium cursus*), and their books don't make any money (if they've ever even published a book before), and they're essentially asking for handouts so that they can "perform and produce their art" (heavy emphasis on the quotation marks; so much emphasis, in fact, that the quotation marks utterly negate the collective denotation of the signifiers they enclose and subjugate). According to Wikipedia:

> Kickstarter is an American-based private for-profit company founded in 2009 that provides

tools to raise funds for creative projects via crowd funding through its website.

Kickstarter has funded a diverse array of endeavors, such as films, music, stage shows, comics, journalism, video games, and food-related projects. People cannot invest in Kickstarter projects to make money. They can only back projects in exchange for a tangible reward or one-of-a-kind experience, like a personal note of thanks, custom T-shirts, dinner with a writer, or initial production run of a new product.

Dinner with a writer. This is grounds for a Kickstarter campaign? If that's the case, I'm setting one up myself to fund the research and composition of *Douglass: The Lost Autobiography*, even though I will be finished with the book long before the official launch of the campaign. I have enough money to live comfortably, with all of the bourgeois accoutrements, embellishments and superfluities I require, but enough is never enough. State-of-the art HGH, creatine, amino acids, etc. aren't cheap, and while I circumvent bottom-of-the-barrel performance-enhancing supplements, I don't buy the VIP brands either. I want the stuff that Hugh Jackman uses to get into shape for his Wolverine movies. My Kickstarter campaign, then, will ultimately assist in the continued transformation of my body (and hence my writing) into a masterful, chiseled-from-onyx "work of art." Whoever contributes the most will have the opportunity to buy me dinner at Dorsia in Chicago or maybe Joël Robuchon's place at the MGM in Las Vegas. Whoever contributes more than, say, $100 will be sent a "personal note of thanks" (form letter) as well as the "tangible reward" of an autographed T-Shirt with a picture of me on the front posing like Richard Roundtree on a promotional poster for *Shaft*. I'm serious.

CHAPTER 46

When the sun sets over the neon sign of the Blue Swallow Motel, the evangelicals say they can see angels sputtering across the chloride sky like ancient zeppelins of war. This happens in times of great doubt, they say, and even when the angels plunge into the horizon like flaming kamikazes, their faith, while jeopardized, never strays from the arena of steel and mortar.

CHAPTER 47

At least one chapter per minute now. My stories will be on soon. It's Sunday evening. I don't have cable or satellite TV. I pirate all of the channels and I pirate them all in HD. Done with 20 seconds to spare.

CHAPTER 48

Still in the motel. 20 goto 10.

CHAPTER 49

It was 10 p.m.

I hadn't put gas in the Mini Cooper for days, but this custom-made job gets, like, 90 miles to the gallon and I hardly ever have to fill it up. I can almost feel the car pleading with me not to fill it up, ever, out of some compulsion to please me and save me money, even if, no matter what, it would eventually run out of gas and come to a slow, quiet stop.

My wife and I drove all day and finally we got to the Blue Swallow Motel.

I don't think I could have taken five more minutes in the car with her. She gets in these moods. Mostly regarding me. But sometimes regarding my writing. Often both.

The whole ride she complained about how this isn't a real novel. I kept telling her she's right, I know, it's a biography, not a completely accurate biography, but a biography nonetheless, and really it's a kind of autobiography, and it's not as mean and trivial and snooty as you keep saying, even though I'm writing it at the speed of light. So forth. She kept harping on *Douglass: The Lost Autobiography* not being a real novel, though, so I acquiesced for her sake and said, "What is a real novel? Something with more words than this—yes. Something that's written crappier than this—absolutely. Something that does the same thing as every other novel—obviously. Something that bores me to sleep—definitely. So forth. Yes, you're right. It's not a real novel. Lucky for everybody."

"You're damn right it's not a real novel," retorted my wife. "Not only that: it's juvenile. That goes for all of the books in your Angry Bland Man trilogy."

"Black. It's Black. It's the Angry Black Author trilogy. You said that on purpose."

"People say things on purpose. Whatever. You used the word 'doggystyle' in *Freud: The Penultimate Biography*. That's a little boy word. You're a little boy."

"I like to keep in touch with where I came from."

"Well I just think you're not trying."

"I know I'm not trying. That's why I'm going to win. That's the point."

"Point or no point or counterpoint—that doesn't make it right. Or resonant. Grow up and write a real novel."

"I've written real novels. That's also part of the point."

"Aren't all your quote-unquote *real novels* quote-unquote *unfinished*? Hence not real novels either. Maybe you'll write a real novel when you get older and become a man."

"I'm a man."

"Didn't you have Spaghetti-Os for lunch?"

"Spaghetti-Os with franks. That's different. Anyway I like Spaghetti-Os. You can like Spaghetti-Os and be, like, a man. Men eat Spaghetti-Os. They're good. It's not like I eat them all the time. Once a week at most. Cheat days, like."

We checked into our room. I spent about an hour thinking about things.

"Would you shut up already?" said my wife, eyes glued to a tablet.

I cocked my head. Did I even say anything?

"Was I speaking out loud?"

"You're always speaking out loud! That's the problem. One among many." She dropped the tablet on the bed, got up and started unpacking our clothes.

I poured myself a complimentary whiskey. Wild Turkey. Pretty good motel. "I can't help it if my Monkey's got a big mouth. Give him a break. Signifyin(g) is the only thing he knows how to do."

My wife eyeballed me. "Better stay up in dem trees."

I said, "Well if you don't like it then just divorce me already. Geez."

"I've tried. You won't let me." She bent over and put some socks in a drawer.

I sat on the bed and sipped my whiskey.

A few minutes later I replied, "You're just not trying hard enough. Man you look good. Come over here, ok? Seriously. Come here. No? Oh calm down. You know I'm just kidding. About everything. Well ok I'm not kidding.

Does it really matter? Seriously come here. You know I love you. Honey? I'll try harder. You'll see. All right? It won't take much. Honey? Honey? All I have to do is lift a finger. There. Look at that finger. Now I'm a man. All right honey? I won't eat Spaghetti-Os anymore. Is that what this is about? It's a cheat day. I can eat anything. Ok? Come here all right? I'll be good. All right? I'll change. All right? All right? Seriously. All right? All right? All right? All right? All right?"

CHAPTER 50

Rampant disinterestedness as aesthetic *idée fixe*. Check out Flaubert. Then return to Kant. Like I said, everything ends up at Kant and more or less stays there with the occasional regression to Plato and so forth.

CHAPTER 51

There's a film called *Harlan*.

The full title is *Harlan: In the Shadow of Jew Süss*.

Here's its description on Netflix:

Documentarian Felix Moeller profiles one of Nazi Germany's most notorious—yet largely forgotten—filmmakers in this penetrating bio-graphical portrait of Veit Harlan, best known for directing the anti-Semitic 1940 propaganda film Jew Süss. Rare footage sheds light on Harlan's method and motivations, but interviews with his descendants reveal conflicted emotions about his tainted cinematic legacy.

I just discovered the film on a break from reruns of *The Incredible Hulk* starring Bill Bixby and Lou Ferrigno. For some reason, it was in my **More Like Afro Samurai** queue. I should have mentioned it in some capacity in *Hitler: The Terminal Biography*, but this is better than nothing.

CHAPTER 52

Only when you abandon the supremacy of the *Genital-primat* will you even approach a viable (let alone stylized and compelling) *Weltanschauung*. The same goes for the abject. You too can sing the American Dream. So much depends upon the weather and the color of chicken-feathers. (*Sotto voce*: I am not trying to seduce you.)

The kitchen explodes before the dining room . . .

CHAPTER 53

The covers for my Angry Black Author trilogy are brilliantly designed by artist, author, musician and sous chef Matthew Revert, who I work with on countless other projects these days. I don't know whether or not he intended to produce a certain collective effect, but if you juxtapose the covers in chronological order, you will perceive a kind of Descent of Man aesthetic, beginning on the left with Hitler, who stands tall, and moving from Freud to Douglass, who, one after the other, sit lower and lower on the covers and are vaguely hunched over. Clearly Hitler's pose is compensatory. I wonder what sort of posture Freud and Douglass had; I want to tell them to push back their shoulders and sit up straight, as my parents reminded me to do when

I was a child, rendering the posture of my adult self so wildly neutral and non-scoliotic that I could probably charge people to observe me occupying a chair. All three figures obviously need to get in the gym and add lean muscle to their physiques, but that's beside the point. In terms of what this so-called Descent of Man represents for the figures in question as well as the ABA trilogy, I like to think of it as more of an Ascension of Man, progressing from the Worst (Hitler) to the Best (Douglass) through the sieve of the Pathological (Freud). This is essentially the framework of the human condition. Thus spake Nietzsche: "Man is something that must be overcome." By which he meant: "The human subject must be deconstructed." In other words: "Fuck the sociocultural matrix that inter-pellates you. Rise above that matrix with a Will to Power and become a Free Spirit (i.e., a thoroughbred *Artiste*)." Thus will you become the best you can be. And nobody is the best they can be. Hiter might blame this on the Jews. Freud might blame it on guilt culture and the specter of aggression. Douglass might blame it on the suppression of knowledge. Nietzsche might blame it on people who aren't Nietzsche. I might blame it on people who can't control their eating habits and don't work out with free weights on a regular basis. You might blame it on infidelity or reality TV or *stachybotrys chartarum* (black mold). Whatever the case, SUBJECTIVITY ALWAYS WINS.

CHAPTER 54

I am the premier African American scholar, philologist, and pedagogue-in-chief at the Ludavico Campus of the University of Fostoria. Twice a year I teach a survey in African American literature. Usually I begin with Venture Smith, Olaudah Equiano, or Phillis Wheatley, but sometimes I get caught up teaching students how to read a syllabus for the first two or three weeks, so I just start with Frederick Douglass.

Once I was teaching Frederick Douglass's first autobiography, *Narrative of the Life of Frederick Douglass*. The second and third autobiographies, *My Bondage & My Freedom* and *Life & Times of Frederick Douglass*, are far more interesting yet far too long for my students, whereas

Narrative of the Life weighs in at about the same length as *Douglass: The Lost Autobiography*, the perfect length for any book in short-attention-span culture. "For this assignment," I explained, "I'd like you to compose a character profile of Frederick Douglass. We have discussed character profiles in detail, and chapter six in our textbook contains several samples that you should read, study, and use as templates for your own work. Textual support should include the primary source, of course, as well as at least three secondary sources that you should procure from the MLA International Bibliography. This assignment should be three to four pages long."

A student raised his hand. "Do we need to have secondary sources?"

I said, "For this assignment, I'd like you to compose a character profile of Frederick Douglass. We have discussed character profiles in detail, and chapter six in our textbook contains several samples that you should read, study, and use as templates for your own work. Textual support should include the primary source, of course, as well as at least three secondary sources that you should procure from the MLA International Bibliography. This assignment should be three to four pages long."

Another student raised her hand. "How long does it have to be?"

I said, "For this assignment, I'd like you to compose a character profile of Frederick Douglass. We have discussed character profiles in detail, and chapter six in our textbook contains several samples that you should read, study, and use as templates for your own work. Textual support should include the primary source, of course, as well as at least three secondary sources that you should procure from the MLA International Bibliography. This assignment should be three to four pages long."

Another student raised his hand. "Can you explain what you mean by, uhm . . . cataract profile?"

I said, "For this assignment, I am going to catch a chicken and kill it right here in front of you. I've never caught a chicken but I think I can do it. I wonder what a chicken feels like with its feathers on. And is there a special way to kill it? You just wring its neck and yank its head off, right?"

Another student raised his hand. "Can the profile be less than three pages?"

I said, "I am a meat puppet. I am a long dangling thing. I am the Underneath. I am stronger than fleas. I once climbed a Hyperion redwood and talked to God. '*Va te faire foutre, trouduc!*' God said. I fell."

Another student raised her hand. "Can you, like, tell me who is Frederick Douglass?"

I opened a flask of vodka and said, "I gotta admit I really don't like how I feel after a cheat day. I swear I go crazy or something." Sip. "I think I'm allergic to wheat, maybe starch. Last night I ate a large bowl of pasta and Swedish meatballs for dinner and for dessert I ate a peanut butter and jelly sandwich and a bag of potato chips." Sip. "Afterwards I was so bellyful, so deranged with Excess." Sip. "I wasn't meant to eat like that. Nobody is. That's why I only cheat once a month now—to remind myself how much I hate it and how much it negatively affects me." Sip. Sip. Sip. "I encourage you to do likewise. Indeed. Rest assured I can't wait to eat good today."

Another student raised his hand. "What are good foods to eat?"

I closed the flask of vodka and said, "Now we're getting somewhere, folks. But let's not jump ahead of ourselves. First things first. When you lift weights, you need to do so in a slow and controlled fashion. This is especially important for beginners . . ."

CHAPTER 55

Flying is forever.
They don't power out—
never.

This is engraved onto the hatchback of my Mini Cooper.
My nephew said it to my daughter once, explaining
something. I arranged his words in the form of a haiku.
I don't know what they mean. I like the sound of them.
I really like they way they look together in this organiza-
tional pattern. Beneath the haiku, on my bumper, is the
address of my flash website for the third and final book in
my scikungfi trilogy, *The Kyoto Man*, currently available
from Raw Dog Screaming Press:

WWW.THEKYOTOMAN.COM

Tax purposes.

The Kyoto Man is perhaps my finest work of fiction. It took me five years to write. I would be hard pressed to out-author its author. Once I finish a book, it's not long before I regret its existence. Soon I come to despise it. This hasn't happened yet with *The Kyoto Man*. Here's the cover description of the novel:

In the wake of the Stick Figure War, civilization lapsed into obscurity. Fallout ravaged the fabric of space and time. History digested reality and reality exhumed the future as survivors tried and failed to create a new beginning . . . Amid the chaos, one man experiences a terminal affliction, a revolution of the self: the chronic transformation into the city of Kyoto, Japan. Each transformation further plunges the world into darkness, but he's helpless against the lethal clockwork of his body, his psyche, his mindscreens—and nothing, not even Fate itself, can stop him from becoming God . . . In the third and final installment of the Scikungfi trilogy after *Dr. Identity* and *Codename Prague*, acclaimed author Washington Bailey composes a narrative grindhouse that combines elements of science fiction and horror with pop culture and literary theory. Erudite, ultraviolent, and riotously satirical, *The Kyoto Man* reminds us how, at every turn, reality is shaped by the forces that destroy it.

CHAPTER 56

Douglass: The Lost Autobiography is intended to be a guerrilla brand of lazy, out-of-the-lower-corner-of-your-mouth rap initiated by Jay-Z. Lesser known as Shawn Corey Carter, Jay-Z commands a net worth of approximately $450 million dollars and is married to Beyoncé, lesser known as Beyoncé Giselle Knowles-Cartera, who, just as Samson gained strength from his hair, gains strength from the curvature of her hips and the ability to make her voice go up and down with a marvelous trill. Jay-Z's strength, of course, comes from "not trying," i.e., from "being lazy" when he raps. Together this power-couple represents the apogee of the American Dream; they are everything everybody wants to be, the epicenter of collective desire and wish-fulfillment fantasy. This is why *Douglass: The Lost Autobiography* (and, *ipso facto*, *Freud: The Penultimate Biography* and *Hitler: The Terminal Biography*) will succeed.

Now some final words about Bram Stoker.

CHAPTER 57

There was a beautiful girl that Irish bodybuilder Bram Stoker used to love and he sang to her all the time in this really gorgeous-sounding, like, Gaelic voice. It meant so much to him.

That had been around twenty years ago.

Now the girl was out-of-shape and old-looking and Republican and she abused her kids and neglected her pets and she was as racist as she was homophobic and xenophobic. Their past meant nothing to Bram. The singing and his love were just a constellation of bugstains on the windshield of his memory. Thus the inspiration to enfang Vlad the Impaler.

Thus the inspiration for all of our lost autobiographies.

CHAPTER 58

I'm going to send this manuscript to my publisher. As is. It's not quite 15,000 words. I haven't revised it at all. I don't want to write anymore if I don't have to. In the next chapter I'll let you know what my publisher thinks.

CHAPTER 59

There are some strengths and some weaknesses. Obvious strengths include your token Hörnblowér prose, your rapier wit, your knowledge of bodybuilding and Lacanian psychoanalysis, etc. Obvious weaknesses include a lack of sex, a lack of believable characters, a lack of plot, a lack of transparent prose, prose that oscillates between gibbous jargon and rubberneck colloquy for no apparent reason, etc. In other words, business as usual. But I got to tell you there's something about this manuscript. Plan on flying out tomorrow morning and we'll talk more about it. Bring your gardening shoes and an extra set of nitrile gloves, if you have them. We only have one pair.

CHAPTER 60

A writer sent me his debut novel. He kept emailing me to see if I had read it. He knew I was a professor of How to Tell the Truth at the Ludavico Campus of the University of Fostoria. He may have even read my books. He may have even liked them.

I think he asked if he could send his book to me at a writing convention and I said yes. Unless I'm in the hotel gym, I'm always drunk at writing conventions and I tell everybody anything they want to hear. I'll convince you you're god if you corner me at a writing convention.

A year went by. I must have received fifty emails from the writer. The first one was a long, tedious *apologia pro vita sua*. The last one was in textspeak: "pls."

Whenever I absently (i.e., drunkenly) invite writers into my home, as it were, they go away after they discover that my veins contain bugjuice. And watered-down bugjuice at that. Abject silence does wonders.

I got the feeling that this writer wanted to live with me, forever, no matter what.

I sent him an email. I told him thank you, etc., but I only read literary theory (preferably Lacan) and books I review for academic journals (primarily science fiction criticism). I haven't read a new novel since college. I don't like fiction. I don't like paragraphs and sentences and indirect objects and punctuation marks. So forth. It was a long email. It seemed to do the trick, though, because I never heard from the writer again, and that worked out really, really well for me.

CHAPTER 61

Enough about writers and writing. You get the point.

As for bodybuilding, I have indicated that I own a home gym, but I belong to a Max Fitness down the road too. They have state-of-the-art equipment, good lighting, and kind mirrors. DO NOT FUCKING APPROACH ME DURING A WORKOUT. I'm happy to talk to you, sign books, sign body parts, take pictures, etc. when I'm done. But when I'm in the gym, I'm in the zone, every time, from beginning to end, a fair price to pay for the grooves and striations, the bulges and veinscapes that provide my frame with its shatterproof identity. I don't care if the gym is exploding. My limbs won't burst asunder until I'm done with my last rep.

CHAPTER 62

A final point about writers and writing. (And no, it doesn't have anything to do with the Marquis de Sade, although that's who I'm thinking about right now, particularly *Philosophy in the Bedroom*, which, in "Kant avec Sade," a short essay in *Écrits*, Lacan argues "completes" and "yields the truth" of Kant's *Critique of Practical Reason*, published in 1788, eight years before the publication of Sade's *Philosophy*.)

Forget about the dress.

CHAPTER 63

As I mentioned near the beginning of *Hitler: The Terminal Biography*, "Lacanian psychoanalysis is a nice way to enter into a discussion of identity and the politics of subjectivity but perhaps not the best vehicle to jumpstart a biography, or a novel, or any 'entertaining' book-length project." Likewise is it "perhaps not the best vehicle" to end (or start to end) a novel, but that's precisely what we're going to do, if only to frame the Angry Black Author trilogy with thick and brassy edges, and if only because the unconscious, god of everything that creeps and flies, is structured like a language.

Jacques Lacan removed a cigarette from a fresh pack and lit it. "Hey, you there!" he cried. But he was talking

about himself. He said it *en Français.* "*Hé, ta geule!*"
Arrête. That didn't mean the same thing. Anyway he didn't
even smoke and he had never bought a pack of cigarettes
in his life. He wondered where they came from. But he
didn't like to be wasteful so he smoked the entire pack as
his students looked on. Then he returned to his lecture,
"On Nonsense and the Structure of God," the ninth entry
in his third seminar on the psychoses.

After class a few students tried to talk to him, but Lacan
wasn't feeling particularly well. He grabbed his manservant
and told him to get him a stimulant.

"*Un tonique?*" said Jacques-Alain Miller.

"No, a stimulant," said Lacan. "Just pull up the car and
open the door please. My goodness."

Miller squealed out of the parking garage and drove
around campus but he couldn't find his mentor. Lacan
hadn't been where he was supposed to be. Miller found
him curled up around a stop sign, shivering in his overcoat.
His big white pompadour had fallen apart and there was
soot in it.

Alarmed, Miller carried Lacan into the Lincoln Town
Car and started driving. "Where to, Boss?"

"Do you have a cigarette?" asked Lacan. "I think I have
become addicted. At this moment I feel about cigarettes
just as I feel about feasible erogenous zones: I must possess
them—I must, as Hemingway says, *become one with the
bull.* I shouldn't have smoked that whole pack. Perhaps an
apéritif." He poured himself a glass of sherry. He drank it
and poured another one. "That may have done the trick."
He slumped back in his seat and said, "Don't miss that
light. It's yellow. You can make it."

Miller didn't make it. He tried, but the car in front of him stopped and he had to stop too.

Lacan burst out of the Town Car and stormed into traffic. He got sideswiped by a Mini Cooper that spun him around but it didn't do any major damage and he got to the other side of the street. He kept going. As always, Miller pulled up beside Lacan and rolled down the window and tried to coax his mentor back inside the Town Car. And, as always, Lacan ignored him and plodded forward, clenched fists swinging at a good rhythm. After awhile Miller stopped shouting and pleading and rolled up the window. Everybody was honking their horns at him to go faster, exasperating him, but he kept following Lacan, and he brought the Town Car to complete stops when Lacan would pause to ask people for cigarettes. He smoked a lot at first but the intervals between cigarettes became longer and longer and by the time he had gotten home he had either kicked or forgotten about the habit.

"Home," intoned Lacan, enervated. "Home is where the *hystérie* is."

He wasn't married anymore, and sometimes he forgot if he had been married in the first place. Whatever the case, like all human beings, he enjoyed performativity, especially when it regarded ordinary, everyday things. So he talked aloud as if somebody were listening to him. That's the best way to talk—under the assumption that an audience is always-already present. This ensures that the speaker does not plummet into idle linguistic chasms of signification. This ensures that the speaker is always-already one with the bull.

He ate.

After dinner Lacan put on his pajamas and climbed into bed. It took him ten or fifteen minutes to get to sleep as he reviewed that morning's seminar and identified the places in need of fine-tuning and in some cases total renovation. Then he slipped into unconsciousness and everything was black and loud and metonymic.

CHAPTER 64

The darkest card is always the slipperiest. Nobody likes it in their hand and nobody likes to talk about it. But everybody wants to call it into question. So it goes with the Angry Black Author trilogy. Things were much easier when I was writing about glaciers. They always are.

CHAPTER 65

A man read a book. He liked the book so much he read another book and when he finished it he said to himself man I'm gonna read another book! This went on for awhile. Then he got bored and thought he would try the same thing with something else.

A man turned on a lamp. He liked turning it on so much he turned on another lamp and when the lightbulb exploded he said to himself man I'm gonna turn on another lamp! This went on for awhile. Then all of the lightbulbs exploded and he ran out of replacement bulbs and so he had to forsake the project of turning on lamps.

A man sat down to eat breakfast. He liked what he ate so much he ate lunch and when he finished lunch he said to himself man I'm gonna eat dinner! This went on for awhile. Then he got full and had to find something else to do. There was a lot of time in life. In the long, seemingly endless hallways of time, one must do things in order to cast oneself in the role of *homo erectus*.

A man was walking down a hallway and tripped over a set of dumbbells. He picked them up and did five curls. He liked how it felt so much he tried to do five more curls but he could only do three more and at that point his muscles were bulging like outraged pufferfish. Frightened, he dropped the dumbbells and gave up.

A man sat down to write about his experience with dumbbells. He liked what he wrote so much he wrote about his experience eating breakfast and when he finished that story he wrote about things he did with lamps and books. This brought him full circle. This brought him grief. This brought him dread. Eventually this brought him death.

A man crawled into a coffin and laid there. He liked laying there so much he got into another coffin and when he finished laying in it he said to himself man I'm gonna lie down in another coffin . . .

CHAPTER 66

And now I am reminiscing a better age.

The Jazz Age. Always the Jazz Age.

Skulking down the streets of Harlem in a white flannel suit, silver shirt and gold-colored tie as schized saxophones and cymbals flood into the night, devouring all of the flappers, the zooters, the gatsbys and the gangsters.

Just as all theory backslides into Kant and his predecessors, so does the social backslide to the Jazz Age. Every time. Even that which existed prior to the Jazz Age backslides into the Jazz Age.

Suddenly the dialectic becomes palpable, physical.

I fall into history and my smartphone falls onto the leather cushion of the Deco lounger in my home theater, smart enough by now to write the rest of *Douglass: The Lost Autobiography* on its own.

The wallscreen skips and coughs as I fizzle into view.

I'm standing outside the mansion. It's lit from tower to cellar.

I go inside. It's time for a cocktail. Beefeater martinis around the house. That was F. Scott Fitzgerald's hallmark brand of liquid courage—straight up with an olive. There's an author who knew how to drink a drink, although he had no concept of fitness and proper nutrition. We forgive him for now. We'll save the next lesson for the Afterparty.

CHAPTER 67

Frederick Douglass strode across the temple and shook hands with the President of the United States. "It is very nice to finally meet you, sir," said the President. They were on the front porch of the Lincoln Memorial. Thousands of weary souls stood in and around the reflecting pool. Dark, four-story speakers loomed on either side of the monument like Slender Men.

"My father was a white man," said Douglass, leaning into the microphone.

"I know. It is an unfortunate and horrible thing that was done to you and your people. I hope we can make amends somehow. I think I was unprepared for war," said the President, leaning into the microphone.

"This mode of treatment is a part of the whole system of fraud and inhumanity of slavery. It is so. The mode here adopted to disgust the slave with freedom, by allowing him to see only the abuse of it, is carried out in other things," said Douglass, leaning into the microphone.

"You misunderestimate me. You are a free man. I can assure you that I'm telling you the truth. I want to help. I want to make this thing right, and good, and cheerful, and blessed, and tolerable. I've been in the Bible every day since I've been President," said the President, leaning into the microphone.

"For all slaveholders with whom I have ever met, religious slaveholders are the worst. I have found them the meanest and basest, the most cruel and cowardly, of all others," said Douglass, leaning into the microphone.

"Yesterday, you made note of my—the lack of my talent when it came to dancing. But nevertheless, I want you to know I danced with joy. Please consider the prospect of futurity. In time these wounds will heal over. But I'm telling you there's an enemy that would like to attack America, Americans, again. There just is. That's the reality of the world. And I wish him all the very best," said the President, leaning into the microphone.

Serrated pause. "To be the friend of the one is of necessity to be the enemy of the other," said Douglass, leaning into the microphone.

"And they have no disregard for human life," said the President, leaning into the microphone.

"It proves at least that the white slave can sink as low in the scale of humanity as the black one," said Douglass, leaning into the microphone.

There was an awkward silence. The President didn't know how to respond. Then, nervously:

"I know that human beings and fish can coexist peacefully. I remember meeting a mother of a child who was abducted by the North Koreans right here in the Oval Office," said the President, leaning into the microphone.

"Fish? North Koreans? I have already intimated that my condition was much worse," said Douglass, leaning into the microphone.

"Of course. I didn't mean to suggest otherwise. Look. I promise you I will listen to what has been said here. Even though I wasn't here," said the President, leaning into the microphone.

"You are a cruel man, hardened by a long life of slaveholding. You have at times taken great pleasure in whipping slaves. You whip them to make them scream," said Douglass, leaning into the microphone.

"Fair enough. But rarely is the question asked: Is our children learning? The fact is they are learning. They will learn. They have to learn. But they may not learn and that's ok. I'm the commander. See, I don't need to explain. I do not need to explain why I say things. That's the interesting thing about being President," said the President, leaning into the microphone.

A bright blast of fireworks coincided with hysterical applause. Then the bass and the kettledrums began to thump, and the synthesizer accomplished an erratic staccato, and the preacher's techno-ambient voice slithered out of the loudspeakers.

"They'll church you if you sip a dram and damn you if you steal a lamb," said Douglass, leaning into himself.

CHAPTER 68

I wanted to end with that last chapter. Originally I did a
faceoff between the President (a.k.a. George W. Bush) and
Frederick Douglass (a.k.a. Jay-Z), ripping off lyrics from
the song "No Church in the Wild" and sticking them into
Douglass's maw, but there are copyright issues (according
to eHow.com, you can only use lyrics 90 years after they
are published, or 120 years after their creation), and my
publisher has a fit whenever I try to skirt copyrights. So the
chapter doesn't really work like I want it to, and I had to
make Douglass eat his own words, so to speak, arrogating
select passages from *Narrative of the Life* (no problem
with copyright there). Also my wife wants me to end on
a different note. She thinks it's too crass and risqué. And

nowhere near as clever as I would have it. I don't know why I let her read and edit my work sometimes.

CHAPTER 69

Attention.

What you are reading right now is not my writing but my husband's writing.

I haven't read one word of his Angry Blasé Argonaut trilogy and I certainly haven't written any of it.

And I don't care what kind of note he ends on as long as he takes care of his domestic chores and picks up the girls from school every day. I drive them, after all, and I give them baths every night too. Also I get their clothes on in the mornings and make their lunches.

Whatever he says I wrote he wrote it himself.

CHAPTER 70

Black. Author. It's the Angry Black Author trilogy. By the way I can't stand how you eat chocolate. The way you bite into it with the front of your teeth and make that chitinous clicking noise.

CHAPTER 71

Whatever. I wonder if you might talk about how you're always writing when you should be tending to the house and the kids and mowing the lawn. It seems like I'm always doing the heavy lifting. I was just on the phone with the editor-in-chief of your publisher and she totally agrees. We both want to have a life too, you know, but we understand that writing is important to you and we want you to be happy. So the thesis of your discussion should clearly underscore how your stories and your novels and your "biographies" are products of our sacrifice. It's the least you can do.

CHAPTER 72

Maybe you'd like to fictionalize the discussion between you and the editor-in-chief for me in the interest of my readers' *jouissance*? Readers like to read fiction when they're reading fiction, after all, instead of reading a gallery of short dissertations on their own mental and physical inadequacies as well as conversations between the author and his wife. It would be weird if I did it. As Kafka says in his fable "The Vulture": "Would you do that for me?"

CHAPTER 73

"I've only got to go home and get my gun," says Donovan Ogg, the multiple award-winning director and filmmaker who had been forsaken, who did not once appear in *Douglass: The Lost Autobiography* yet established a daunting protagonism in *Freud: The Penultimate Biography*, even though he died in *Freud: The Penultimate Biography*. But it's never too late to make a comeback. What better time to make that comeback than at the bitter end?

CHAPTER 74

Donovan Ogg gasped for breath under the weight of his wife. She had not gone to the gym in awhile and she had been eating too many carbs and processed foods. But he didn't want to make her feel badly. He muffled his gasps, and pretended like he was breathing and panting normally.

He made them scrambled eggs with a side of fresh blueberries and raspberries for breakfast. It was early. The kids were still asleep. That's pretty early. The sun had not yet crept over the mountains, but it wasn't dark out.

They ate on the screened-in porch. Afterwards they drank cappuccinos made from their beloved Nespresso machine and listened to the wind in the trees and talked about bad films. It was nice. Donovan couldn't imagine a better way to begin the day. This was utopia. Clear vision, clear conscience, clear desiring-palate, absence of hard thought and berserk wills to power—utopia.

When the drinks had been drunk and the conversation had run its course, Donovan retreated to the basement, to his home theater, with a mind to edit his latest master-piece, an adaptation of the Pulitzer Prize-winning, *New York Times* bestseller *Hitler: The Terminal Biography*.

Nobody ever saw him again.

DOUGLASS
THE LOST AUTOBIOGRAPHY

ABOUT THE AUTHOR

D. HARLAN WILSON is an award-winning, critically acclaimed novelist, short story writer, theorist, editor, historian, publisher and English professor. Visit him online at **DHarlanWilson.com** and **TheKyotoMan.com**.

An icon of true evil, Adolf Hitler is arguably the most important figure of the twentieth century. No one has so patently demonstrated the horrific capabilities of mankind. In *Hitler: The Terminal Biography*, D. Harlan Wilson tracks the life of the infamous monomaniac from struggling artist to mass murderer. Based on more than ten years of archival research and German sociological study, this one-volume account covers ground previously uncharted by other biographers, drawing heavily on newfound diaries, letters, and phonograph recordings of Hitler's closest confidants as well as the Führer himself.

"An extraordinary and masterful work. Wilson has written the biography to end all biographies." **GIDEON JOHNSON PILLOW,** Professor of History and Chair of African-American Studies at the University of Fostoria

www.RawDogScreaming.com

In this unofficial, unauthorized sequel to Peter Gay's groundbreaking *Freud: A Life of Our Time*, D. Harlan Wilson reveals a side of the man that has proven too disturbing and risqué for past biographers. Based on newly recovered diaries, microfiche, letters, and secret tape recordings, *Freud: The Penultimate Biography* recounts the daring sexual exploits of the father of psychoanalysis. Once considered to be impotent by the age of forty, if only according to the written testimonies of his wife, Freud is now revealed as an uncompromising flâneur, the figurehead of masculine sexuality and phallic prowess that everybody knew he was. It is a dangerous and at times shocking chronicle that puts the very nature of desire on trial.

"Wilson's torrid biography of Sigmund Freud has quickly become my fondest guilty pleasure. And I have many guilty pleasures." **JOHN SAPPINGTON MARMADUKE**, Professor of Psychology and Men's Studies at the University of Fostoria

www.RawDogScreaming.com

www.ingramcontent.com/pod-product-compliance
Lightning Source LLC
Chambersburg PA
CBHW030347180626
46812CB00007B/2790